The Girl Who Lived with the Bears

Retold by BARBARA DIAMOND GOLDIN

Illustrated by ANDREW PLEWES

Gulliver Books   Harcourt Brace & Company   San Diego   New York   London

Text copyright © 1997 by Barbara Diamond Goldin
Illustrations copyright © 1997 by Andrew Plewes

Library of Congress Cataloging-in-Publication Data
Goldin, Barbara Diamond.
The Girl Who Lived with the Bears/Barbara Diamond
Goldin; illustrated by Andrew Plewes.—1st ed.
p. cm.
"Gulliver Books."
Summary: In this retelling of a traditional tale of
the Pacific Northwest, a young girl is captured by
the Bear People after insulting them.
ISBN 0-15-200684-2
1. Indians of North America—Northwest, Pacific—
Folklore. 2. Bears—Northwest, Pacific—Folklore.
[1. Indians of North America—Folklore. 2. Bears—
Folklore. 3. Folklore—Northwest, Pacific.] I. Plewes,
Andrew, 1964–   ill. II. Title.
E78.N77G64   1997
398.24'52974446'089970795—dc20   95-7538

First edition

F E D C B A

Printed in Singapore

*Special thanks to Bill Holm
for his comments on the text and artwork.*

For Lon
—B. D. G.

For my family
—A. P.

*I*T WAS THE TIME when we still knew that animals could be people—eagle people, salmon people, bear people. They could shed their feathers, scales, and skins as they wished. At home in their own villages, far from our watchful eyes, the animals we hunted, feared, and admired looked just like we do.

We knew some of the proper songs and dances and ceremonies that we know now, but we were still learning the ways of living with the animal people. We learned some of these ways through a very unlikely teacher—a haughty and spoiled young girl of the Raven clan.

It was summer. Then, as now, wild berries grew
thickly all over the mountainside, and even those of noble birth had
many tasks to do. The haughty young girl, who was a chief's daughter,
moved among the berry bushes with two of her friends, picking and
talking and laughing.

"And what was wrong with the last one?" one friend teased the
girl. "He was so handsome."

"Not good enough for your parents?" teased the other. "They
will never find a husband for you!"

"They will," answered the girl. "And he will be—" But just then she tripped and fell into some muddy bear tracks on the trail. All the berries spilled out of her basket.

"Those bears!" she complained loudly as she picked herself up. "This isn't the first time I've soiled my clothes because of them. What a nuisance they are. Always leaving tracks. Droppings. Eating the berries—"

"*Sh,*" whispered one of her friends in alarm. "You mustn't talk about the bears so."

"It will anger them," said the other, looking about.

"We'd better go," said the first. "Come on." And the girl's friends started down the trail. They sang songs as they walked so the bears would hear them and know how much they honored them.

"Those two," mumbled the girl. "They would jump at the wind." And even though it was late in the day, she stopped to pick more berries to replace the spoiled ones.

She had almost filled her basket again when suddenly—SNAP!—the strap broke and the basket fell to the ground. All her new berries tumbled out. The young woman groaned.

It was growing dark, and she began to long for the comfort of her friends' talk, even for their loud singing. Leaving the berries behind, she returned to the trail. As she walked, she heard the soft rustle of snapping branches. Someone, something, was coming.

In a moment she could see two men. They walked quietly, with confidence. The taller one was quite handsome.

"We've been sent to help you," he said. "Let me carry your basket."

"Thank you," she said. She was relieved and thought that perhaps her parents had gotten word that she needed help.

As they walked, the two men talked and joked. The girl enjoyed their company and did not notice how they headed up the mountain, not down.

At last they came to a village.

"But this is not my village," the girl said.

"No, it is mine," the tall man said. "Wait for me here while I talk with my uncle." He pointed to a spot outside the great lodge in the very center of the village.

The girl stood there, confused and growing angry. *Handsome or not,* she thought, *he shouldn't keep a chief's daughter waiting.*

Finally, two men came out of the great lodge. Their short hair showed that they were slaves. *Now I will be treated with some respect,* the girl thought. *Perhaps they will ask if I am hungry or tired. . . .* But to her surprise and dismay, the slaves grabbed her arms and dragged her inside a small dark shed. They left her there and blocked the only doorway with a large boulder.

The girl was stunned. *There must be a mistake,* she thought. She began to bang on the door.

"That will do you no good," said a high, squeaky voice. In the darkness the girl could see no one. She began her banging again. Then she felt a pinch on her arm.

"It is Mouse Woman. Give me some wool and some fat."

The girl stopped her banging. "Mouse Woman, will you help me?"

"For some wool and some fat."

The girl reached for the mountain goat fat she carried to rub on her face and keep her skin smooth, and took some wool from her earrings.

"This is all I have," she said.

Mouse Woman snatched up the wool and the fat—one, two.

"Good," said Mouse Woman. "Now listen to me. You have been taken by the Bear People because of the way you insulted them on the trail. It was the chief, with his magical powers, who made your basket strap break. And it was his nephew who led you here."

"But he didn't look like a bear," said the girl.

"He does when he puts on his bearskin," said Mouse Woman.

"This is all a mistake," insisted the girl.

"You're not listening," Mouse Woman squeaked. "I will tell you what you must do. You must take the copper bracelet on your arm and break it into pieces."

"Not my copper bracelet!" She felt another pinch.

"Whenever you hear a slave push aside the boulder in front of this shed to bring you food, slip a piece of the bracelet under your tongue and keep it there. After you've eaten, say 'I wish to give a gift to your chief.' Then cough up the copper. The bears will think you can turn food into copper, and copper is as precious to them as it is to your people. Perhaps, instead of making you a slave, the chief will let you marry his nephew."

"Marry a bear! Oh, no. I'm going home."

"If you wanted to go home, you should have thought of that sooner," came the squeaky voice. "On the trail. Before you showed such disrespect for the bears. Even one of noble birth ... shows ... respect ..." Mouse Woman's voice trailed off as she scurried away with the wool and the fat.

The young woman sat down on the hard dirt floor. She took off her copper bracelet and fingered it lovingly and sadly. It had been a gift from her parents when she came of age. How far away her parents seemed now.

The next morning, the guards came again. They moved the boulder and told the girl to come outside for her food. She was glad to be in the open air again, even for a few minutes. After she'd eaten, she held out the food bowl and said, "I have a gift for your chief to show how much I honor him." In front of the amazed guards, she coughed up a piece of copper.

Every time the guards came, the girl coughed up copper and repeated her message for the Bear Chief. Finally, after several days, she was taken to his lodge. The great chief sat on a carved wooden seat against the far wall. One bearskin after another hung on the walls of the lodge.

"You are obviously a person of high rank," the chief said. "You can transform slave's food into copper. We have been looking for a bride such as you for my nephew."

The chief gestured to his slaves. "Bring mats for this young woman and my nephew. We will have a wedding feast!"

The girl shuddered at his words. She did not want to marry a man who could change into a bear, but to be a slave would be worse.

The feast that followed was much like the ones in the girl's own village. There was singing and dancing and gift giving. There was an abundance of foods of all kinds—salmon and halibut, bird eggs, crab and clams and wild onions. And, of course, berries.

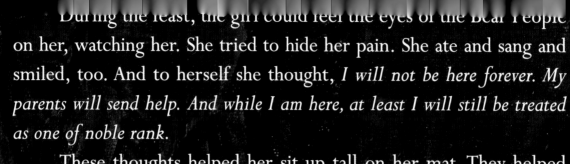

During the feast, the girl could feel the eyes of the Bear People on her, watching her. She tried to hide her pain. She ate and sang and smiled, too. And to herself she thought, *I will not be here forever. My parents will send help. And while I am here, at least I will still be treated as one of noble rank.*

These thoughts helped her sit up tall on her mat. They helped her to glance at the Bear Chief's nephew. He *was* handsome. And his eyes seemed to say "I'm sorry," and "You will be happy here."

From the day of the wedding, the girl joined the life of the Bear People. She knew she must. They watched her always. Were they still angry at her for insulting them, or just distrustful because she was not of their people?

She did the work they expected of her. She helped hang the salmon strips on the drying frames and collected berries. She beat spruce root into strips for the hats and capes she would weave. But all the while she looked for signs of rescue in the woods and bushes and streams. She could not help but long for her lost family. She would see her mother's face looking out at her from among the drying racks, and her youngest brother standing by a tree practicing with his spear. She thought she heard her friends' laughter spilling over into the berry bushes.

The young woman's bear husband was kind to her. His eyes had not lied. Knowing how much she hated seeing him in his bear form, he always assumed his bear shape at a distance. But one day, when she was longing for her family and her home, he gave her a present—a thick brown bearskin of her own. At first, she could not bring herself to touch the skin, let alone put it over her. But she knew this was what her husband wanted her to do, and one afternoon, after he had gone hunting, she lifted the skin from its box and touched it. It was soft and warm and shone in the light. When she covered herself with it, she felt comforted. An affection for her husband and the Bear People enveloped her and she forgot her other life for a time.

As the cold months neared, the sleeping months, the Bear People moved to their winter village, and the young woman knew she would have a child. Would this baby be a bear or a human, she wondered.

When the time came for her to give birth, she had not just one baby, but two! Her twin boys had arms and legs and faces like her people, but they tumbled about, bumping into each other just like any bear cubs. And, like their father, they could put on bearskins and be bears when they wished.

The young woman grew to love her playful sons and she grew to love her handsome bear husband as well. But still something deep within her was often far away, in that place she remembered as home. And at these times, she still secretly longed for rescue.

It was the time when the salmon spawn in the streams that the young woman noticed how quiet her handsome bear husband had become. When she looked at him, she saw a deep sadness in his eyes that she had not seen before.

"Something is troubling you," she said.

"I know things from my dreams," he told her. "I see your youngest brother searching for you."

The young woman looked up, startled. Her husband had never talked of her brothers or her parents or her home, or of her being stolen away.

"We must move from here," he continued. "To a cave above the cliff."

The young woman did as her husband said and moved with him to the cave, all the while feeling a kind of excitement within her. Her brother—how long it had been since she had seen him.

All summer they lived safely in the cave, eating, playing, and sleeping. But when the first snows came, her bear husband once again grew distant, thoughtful, and sad.

"Your brother is very near," he told the young woman. "He is going to find us."

"Please do not kill him," she begged. "He is my brother."

"No, I will not kill my brother-in-law," said her husband. "But I know from my dreams that he must kill me."

As the young woman watched her husband put on his bearskin, she was filled with a great love for him. She was at last able to look at his bear self. But her love for him was mixed with sorrow. "Please, let me talk to my brother."

"No, my wife. You must listen to me," her husband continued. His words reminded her of Mouse Woman's words so many months before.

"It is important that my spirit be set free to return to my people and watch over you and our sons. Tell your brother that once he spears me, he must build a fire and decorate my head with feathers. He must sing the death song that I will sing, and burn my bones in the fire to release my spirit-self.

"Whenever one of your people kills a bear, he must do the same. You and your brother teach them. In this way, my people, the Bear People, will not be angry when one of your people kills a bear for their food.

"Will you do this?"

The young woman looked into her bear husband's eyes, so full of kindness and caring. "I will do as you ask me," she answered. She held him to her, and then took their sons into the cave to wait. Soon she could hear her husband sing his death song. And then she heard her brother's spear find its mark. She felt as if the spear had entered her own heart.

It was the young woman's sobbing that drew her brother into the cave, spear ready, not certain of what he would find.

"Don't!" she called. "It is your sister!"

Her brother dropped his weapon and came to her. She told him all that had happened to her, and together the brother and sister built a fire. They sang her husband's song and released his spirit-self.

The next morning, the young woman, her two sons, and her brother returned home. As she promised, she taught her people her bear husband's songs and ceremonies. She reminded them always to treat the bears, and all animals, with love and great respect, and the village prospered with good hunting and fishing. She knew her bear husband watched over them as he said he would. And neither she nor her sons ever forgot that they were of both villages, the Bear People's and ours.

And now this story ends.

THE STORY of the girl who insulted the bears and was taken to live with them is one of the most popular stories of the native peoples of what is now British Columbia, the Yukon, and Alaska. Over the years it has been told in varying versions by the Haida, Tlingit, Tsimshian, Tagish, Tutchone, and Ahtna peoples.

I first came across this story in a library collection when I lived in Washington State. At the time I was volunteering as a storyteller in a Head Start class on a Lummi reservation and was sharing different kinds of stories with the preschoolers. I went to the library looking for Lummi stories and found a wealth of stories from the native peoples of the region.

The story of the girl who insulted the bears especially appealed to me. Like the young woman in the story, I had just come to live in a totally different place from what I knew as home. I was missing that home and was becoming used to a new life.

In addition, I was impressed with what the story teaches about the delicate balance or harmony that exists between people and animals in the natural world, and the respect people should have for this world. The idea around which the story is built—that animals can shed their skins or scales or feathers and transform into humans, that all is not as it seems—also caught my imagination.

In retelling any story the teller must make choices along the way. With this story I had to decide whether to include just one of the girl's brothers in the search for her or several brothers, as there are in some versions of the tale. I had to consider whether to include her dog, who, in some tellings, hunts for her with her brother, and whether to have this ambivalent young woman help her brother by throwing a snowball that shows him where she is. I decided not to describe the dog or the snowball in the text, but if you look, you will see that Andrew Plewes has included both these traditional elements of the story in his illustrations.

Another choice I faced was where to end the story. After much thought, I chose to end with the young woman returning to her human village—a hopeful moment. Some versions of the story go on to describe further difficulties that she has after returning to her village. They show yet more struggles between animals and humans and what can go wrong between the two when humans show neither respect nor consideration for the animal world and ignore the feelings of both humans and animals. In these versions the girl's brothers urge her to put on her bear coat so they can play a game and pretend to hunt her. But when she reluctantly does this, she looks and acts so much like a real bear that they try to shoot her. She ends up killing her brothers and must leave the human village forever with her two sons. In these versions, the story ends on a more tragic note.

You can find various versions of this young woman's story in *The Girl Who Married the Bear* by Catharine McClellan, *Heroes and Heroines in Tlingit-Haida Legend* by Mary L. Beck, *North American Indian Mythology* by Cottie Burland, and *The Raven Steals the Light* by Bill Reid and Robert Bringhurst. You can find out more about her world from books such as *Indian Art and Culture of the Northwest Coast* by Della Kew and P. E. Goddard, *Monuments in Cedar* by Edward L. Keithahn, and Bill Holm's *Spirit and Ancestor*.

The color illustrations in this book were
done with acrylics and air brush on canvas.
The black-and-white illustrations were done
with pencil crayon on Coquille board.
The display type was hand lettered by Georgia Deaver.
The text type was set in Perpetua.
Color separations by Bright Arts, Ltd., Singapore
Printed and bound by Tien Wah Press, Singapore
This book was printed on totally chlorine-free
Nymolla Matte Art paper.
Production supervision by Stanley Redfern
and Pascha Gerlinger
Designed by Andrew Plewes and Camilla Filancia